Copyright 1910
by
PAUL B. HOEBER
All rights reserved

A FOREWORD.

Since the publication by Ewald and Hoegyes of their epoch making experiments on the semicircular canals of animals and the discovery of the underlying laws of labyrinthine physiology, extensive researches have been conducted at the clinics of Vienna and Berlin on the human labyrinth. While the latter have been but supplemental to the classical work of the above named pioneers, they have served to reduce the subject to a practical basis and to evolve a new and valuable method of diagnosis of conditions hitherto obscure. Nystagmus, which has until recent years, been associated almost entirely with congenital or early acquired optical defects, or in an indefinite way, with lesions of the inner ear, has become one of the most important aids in differential diagnosis and greatly amplified the scope and efficiency of the aurist.

With the exception of a few contributions to

our medical journals by men who have recently visited the Vienna clinics, this is the first attempt to present the subject in detail to the English speaking profession. The subject matter is largely an excerpt of a translation of Dr. Robert Barany's "Physiologie and Pathologie Des Bogengand Apparates (Functions Prufung) Beim Menschen." Much of a statistical nature has been eliminated, as well as detailed descriptions of experimental methods and apparatus. On the other hand, the text has been elaborated and amplified by notes and addenda gathered at the clinics and lectures of Drs. Ruttin, Neumann and Alexander. By means of subdivisions, rearrangements and tabulations it has been sought to present the subject in the simplest, clearest and briefest manner to serve as a guide to both specialist and general practitioner.

The profession is to be congratulated that so finished a scholar and so able a physician and surgeon as Dr. Ibershoff has undertaken this task. I can testify to the author's every qualification for the work. His professional success and his perennial enthusiasm are the delight of his friends. Personally, I have profited much from contact with Dr. Ibershoff. My regret, at this time, is that I could not be more helpful in suggestions regarding this undertaking. I am sure, however, the profession must profit, as I certainly have, from a careful study of the text.

ROYAL S. COPELAND.

58 Central Park, West,
    New York City.

Physiology and Pathology of the Semicircular Canals

ANATOMY.

The vestibular apparatus is composed of the utricle, saccule and three semicircular canals. But little is known at present of the functions of the utricle and saccule, and the details of their anatomy need not concern us here. The position of the semicircular canals with relation to the upright head is, however, of prime importance, and may be demonstrated in the following manner: With the hands in the position shown in Figure I., the palm of the right hand corresponds to the plane of the horizontal semicircular canal, the fingers of the left representing the plane of the right anterior vertical and palm of the left hand, the plane of right posterior vertical canal. The convexity of the three canals coincides with the free borders of the hands, *i. e.*, the horizontal outward, the anterior vertical upward, and the posterior vertical upward and backward. It will be easily seen from this scheme that neither the an-

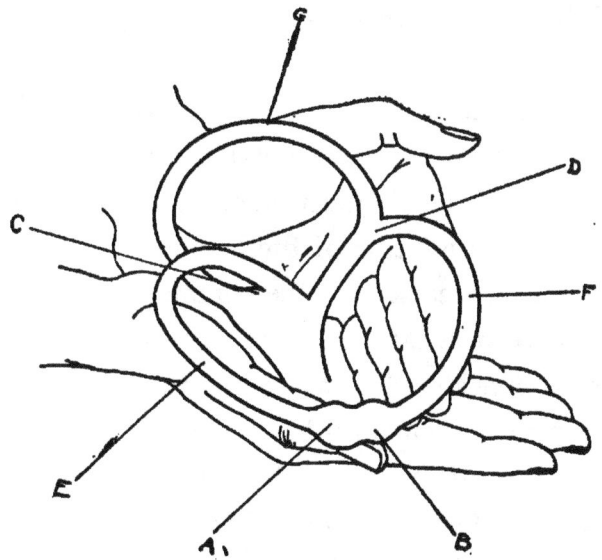

Figure I. Position of the hands to show the relative position of the three semicircular canals (right side). (After Barany.)
A-B—Ampullæ of horizontal and ant. vertical canals. C—Ampulla of post. vertical canal. D—Union of two vertical canals. E, F, G—Arches of horizontal, ant. vertical and post. vertical canals respectively.

terior nor posterior vertical canal lies in the sagittal plane, and that, moreover, both the anterior and posterior canals form an angle of 45 degrees with the sagittal plane. If we consider the relative position of the vertical canals of the right and left sides we will at once see that the right anterior vertical and left posterior vertical lie in the same plane, while the right posterior vertical and the left anterior vertical lie at right angles to this plane. Fig. II.

Of importance is the position of the ampullæ. The ampullæ of the horizontal and anterior vertical canals lie at the junction of these two canals. Note also the position of the ampulla of the posterior vertical canal and the common opening of the two vertical canals into the utricle.

If we consider the position of the canals with relation to the temporal bone, we will recall that the surfaces of the pyramids form approximately a right angle with each other similar to that formed by the fingers in our scheme. The plane of the anterior vertical canal lies crosswise of the petrous portion of the temporal bone, at right angles to its posterior surface and its summit constitutes the eminentia. The posterior vertical canal is nearly parallel to the posterior surface of the petrous bone. Its ampulla is situated near the

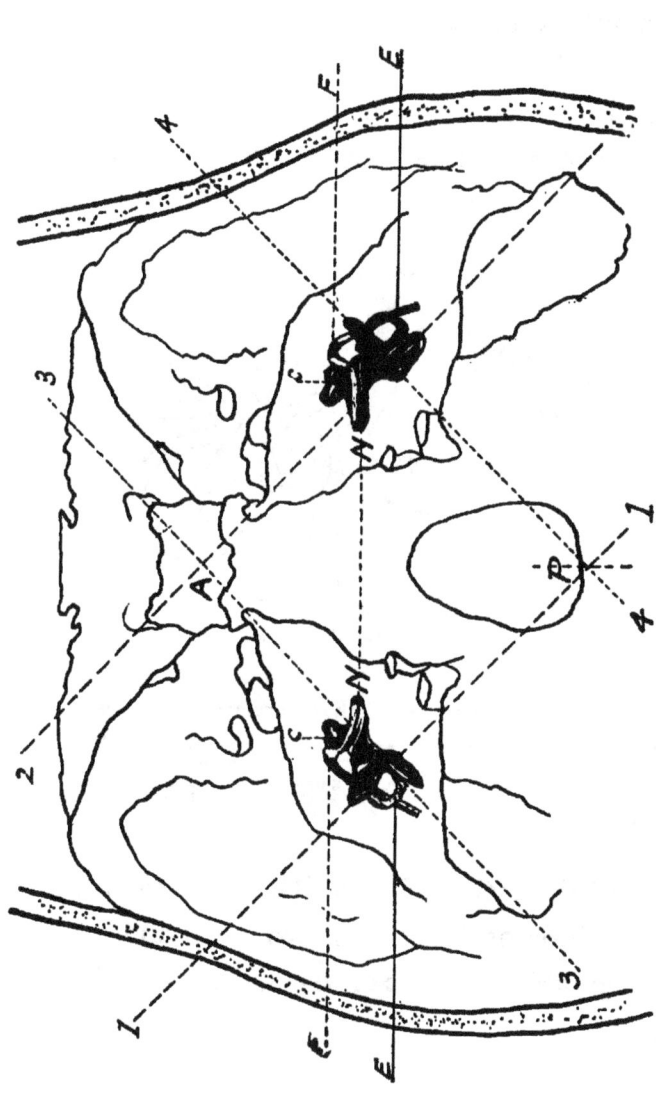

Figure II. Semi-Schematic representation of two labyrinths showing relative positions of semicircular canals to each other. (After Mackenzie.)
N—Seventh and eighth nerves entering int. auditory foramen. C—Cochlea. E—External canal. P—Geniculate ganglion of facial nerve. 1-1—Plane of left ant. vertical canal. 2-2—Plane of right post. vertical, the two being parallel. 3-3—Plane of left post. vertical canal. 4-4—Plane of right ant. vertical canal, the two being parallel.

bulbus venæ jugularis and the fenestra rotunda. The summit of the horizontal canal forms the prominence of the mastoid antrum and its ampulla as well as that of the anterior vertical canal lies directly over the fenestra ovalis and above

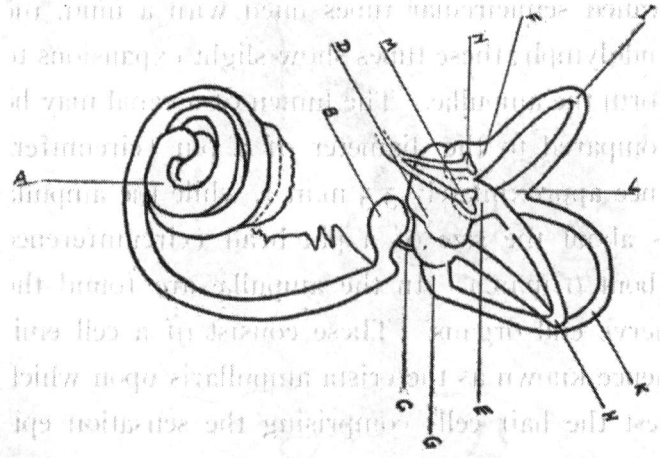

Figure III. Left membranous labyrinth from below. (After Alexander.)
A—Cochlea. B—Sacculus. C—Ductus utriculo saccularis. D—Utricle. E, F, G—Ampullæ of horizontal, ant. vertical and post. vertical canals respectively. H, I, K—Arches of same. L—Union of vertical canals. M—Nerve ending in ampulla of horizontal canal. N—Same in ant. vertical canal.

the bend of the facial. Figure III. represents the relative position of the semicircular canal and the utricle into which they open, the saccule and the cochlea.

HISTOLOGY.

A brief review of the histological structure of the semicircular canals is also essential to an understanding of their functional activity. The canals consist of very small and exceedingly thin-walled semicircular tubes filled with a fluid, the endolymph; these tubes show slight expansions to form the ampullæ. The lumen of a canal may be compared to the diameter of a pin (circumference approximately 3.5 m.m.), while the ampulla is about the size of a pin head (circumference about 6 m.m.). In the ampullæ are found the nerve end organs. These consist of a cell eminence known as the crista ampullaris upon which rest the hair cells comprising the sensation epithelium. Fig. IV. To these are connected the terminal fibres of the nervus vestibularis. The cilia of the hair cells are joined together by a superposed homogeneous mass known as the cupula which extends somewhat beyond the middle of the canal. When the endolymph moves it imparts a jolt to the cupula, which results in an irritation of the cilia of the hair cells. This irri-

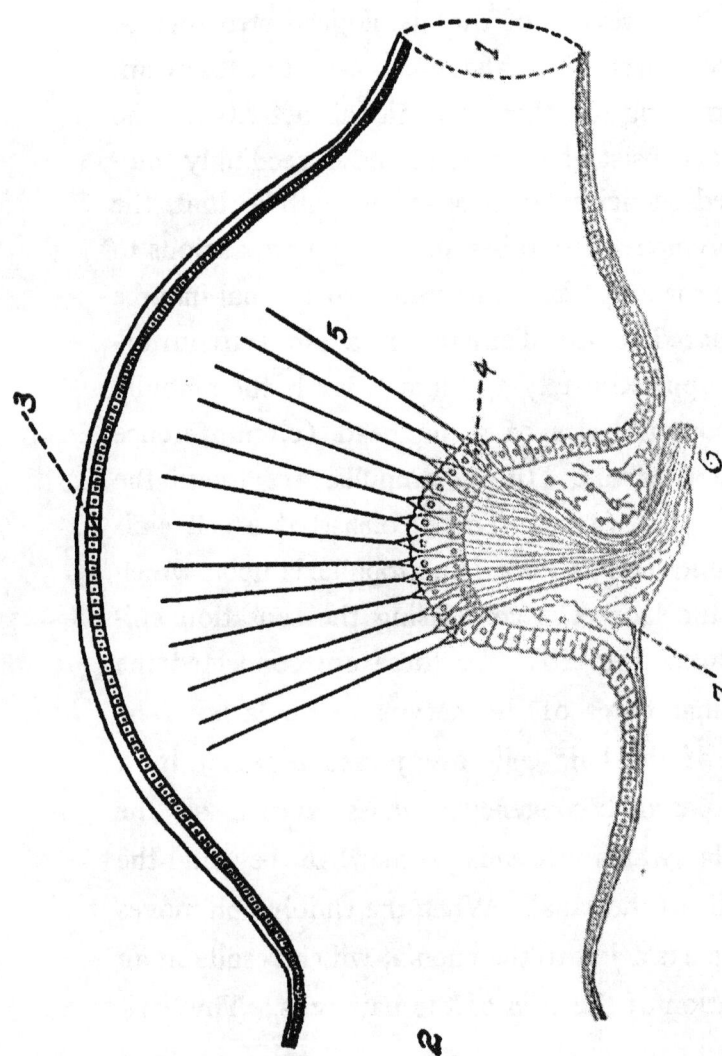

Figure IV. Longitudinal section thru ampulla. (After Hensen.) Schematic. 1.—Junction of canal. 2.—Junction of utricle. 3.—Epithelium. 4.—Neuro-epithelium of crista ampullaris. 5.—Ampullary hairs. 6.—Nerve. 7.—Connective tissue.

tation must be considered as the stimulus, which, conducted to the brain center, causes perception and reflex activity. The vestibular fibres after their interruption in the ganglion vestibulari pass on to the vestibular nerve centers in the medulla oblongata, where they lie in close relation to Deiter's area situated at the junction of the medulla and cerebellum. From this center certain crossed and uncrossed fibres pass along the posterior longitudinal bundles to the oculo-motor center, while others extend downward to the motor cells in the anterior horns of the spinal cord. It is doubtful whether any of the fibres go directly to the cerebral cortex or whether all of them are previously interrupted at the oculo-motor area. Those fibres which stand in relation to the oculo-motor centers effect the reflex movement of the eyes resulting from vestibular irritation. Those passing into the spinal cord cause the disturbances of equilibrium which result from powerful vestibular stimulation. Those fibres which pass to the cerebral cortex effect the perception of movement during the rotating process and the sensation of apparent rotation in the resting body resulting from powerful vestibular excitation.

PHYSIOLOGY.

* The first observations relative to the manifestation of dizziness on rotation were made by Purkinje in 1825. He was afforded ample opportunity for observation among the insane, who, in accordance with the therapeutic method popular at the time, were revolved on a turntable, and noted the fact that ocular nystagmus manifested itself during and immediately following this procedure. Purinje was naturally totally in the dark as to the cause of this manifestation, and attributed the same to centrifugal displacement of the brain.

* About this same time in the year 1824-1825, Flourens published his investigations relative to the sectioning of the semicircular canals in pigeons. Flourens found upon cutting one of the semicircular canals that violent and uncontrollable movements of the head, eyes and the entire body followed in the plane of the canal. From these

observations he deducted the hypothesis that the semicircular canals were the seat of a force which under normal conditions exercised a restraining and controlling influence over bodily movements.

In the year 1870 Goltz first voiced the idea that the semicircular canals were an organ of equilibration which under normal conditions is concerned with the regulation of corporeal balance.

Mach, Breuer and Crum Brown have amplified the knowledge of these canals. The Mach-Breuer theory still stands, although disputed and not proved in detail. Mach and Breuer consider the semicircular canals as an organ for the perception of acceleration during rotation, *i. e.*, they assume that the difference in speed between beginning rotation and after prolonged rotation is appreciated through the agency of the semicircular canals.

Closer investigation relative to the functions of this organ were made by Hoegyes, and more especially by Ewald. The latter developed the technique of his investigation to the highest degree, and we are indebted to him for most conclusive experiments. In one of his experiments he demonstrated most strikingly the facts with which we are concerned. Ewald opened the right osseous horizontal canal; he then made a small puncture toward the smooth end at a distance of several m.m. from the ampulla, and through this

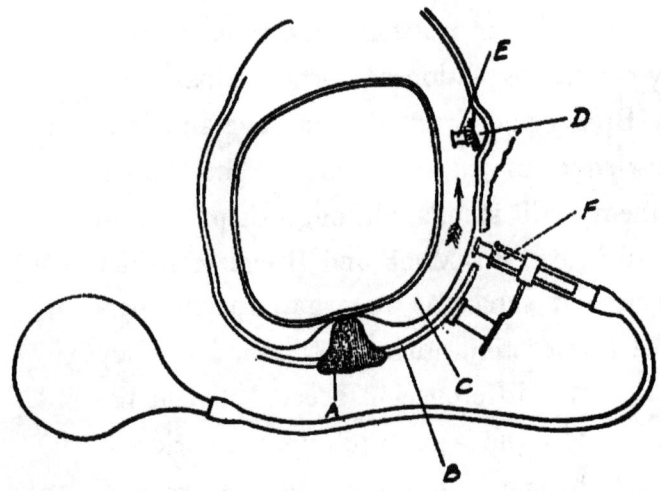

Figure V. A—Plug. B—Bony horizontal canal. C—Lumen of Membranous canal. D—Crista ampullaris. E—Cupula. F—Pneumatic hammer. (After Barany.)

opening inserted a plug which closed the membranous canal at this point. Between the plug and the ampulla Ewald bored a second hole into the bony canal. He then constructed a pneumatic hammer consisting of a small straight capillary tube open at both ends in which glided a glass piston. Fig. V. To the upper end of the glass cylinder was attached a rubber tube equipped with a compression bulb by means of which the air in the cylinder could be compressed or rarified and the hammer forced in and out. The hammer was so placed that when the bulb was compressed it pressed upon the membranous canal between the inserted plug and the ampulla. Because of the closure of the smooth end of the canal the endolymph was compelled to move *toward* the ampulla on compression of the piston, while upon aspiration a movement in the opposite direction was effected.

Upon compression there was regularly observed a slow horizontal movement of the head and eyes to the left, while aspiration was followed by a gradual horizontal movement of the head and eyes to the right.* This experiment demonstrates, therefore, the relationship existing be-

---

*Although excitation of the semicircular canals in animals is productive of a movement of the head as well as of the eyes. such manifestation is found in man only in very exceptional cases. In the human we find only nystagmus of the eyes.

tween a definite motion of the eyes and head and the direction of the endolymph current in a certain canal. In a like manner by experiments upon the vertical canals Ewald was able to produce head and eye movements in their respective planes.

NYSTAGMUS.

*Nystagmus is a simultaneous and associated movement of both eyes. Two types of nystagmus are recognized, viz.: First, the *oscillating* nystagmus in which both movements are equally rapid so that it is manifestly impossible to speak of its direction. Secondly, a so-called *rhythmic* nystagmus in which it is possible to distinguish a slow and a rapid movement. The latter almost always emanates from the vestibular apparatus.

OSCILLATING NYSTAGMUS.

Oscillating nystagmus is essentially an optical nystagmus, *i. e.*, its etiology is always found to be either an early acquired or congenital central visual defect. Central corneal and lenticular opacities or macular defects occurring very early in life lead to the so-called "searching movements" which are merely an attempt to "see around" the obstruction. These searching movements when once established constitute an oscillating nystagmus, although in rare instances they become rhythmic in character. Such a nystagmus may improve with age, but is not susceptible of perfect cure.

Another form of optical nystagmus is that found in miners, compositors, and paper makers, the result of clonic spasm resulting from keeping the eyes in a strained upward position. Change of employment is usually sufficient to correct such a nystagmus. There is also a form of pseudo-nystagmus resulting from hereditary ataxia, multiple sclerosis and other nervous affections, and may be seen occasionally in apparently healthy individuals as a symptom of fatigue or weakness of the ocular muscles.

Oscillating nystagmus is not accompanied by vertigo, cannot be produced experimentally, and, when not occupational, is always of pathological significance and usually a permanent condition.

RHYTHMIC NYSTAGMUS.

Rhythmic nystagmus is almost always bilateral. Only in very exceptional cases has it been found to be unilateral or unequal. It may be produced physiologically, experimentally or pathologically.

OPTICAL.—Physiological rhythmic nystagmus of optical origin is that form produced by looking out of a train window or elevator car or at moving objects, such as a carousal or waterfall. It may also be produced by maintaining the eyes in the extreme lateral position. This form is probably etiologically identical with miner's nystagmus, and results from the strong cerebral impulses to the ocular muscles and the inability of the latter to maintain the excessive contraction.

VESTIBULAR.—Physiological rhythmic nystagmus of vestibular origin is produced by turning the head in any direction. According to Barany a single rotation will suffice for this, even with the eyes closed. When the eyes are open the nystagmus represents a combined optical and vestibular nystagmus; with the eyes closed it is purely vestibular.

Vestibular nystagmus always becomes more

manifest when the eyes are voluntarily turned in the direction of the rapid movement. It becomes weakened or entirely suppressed when gazing in the direction of the slower movement.

We recognize three degrees of nystagmus, viz.: 1. That which can be detected only when the patient looks in the direction of the rapid movement. 2. That which can be perceived when the eyes are directed straight forward. 3. That which is manifest even when the eyes are turned in a direction opposite to the rapid movement.

The direction of a nystagmus is always determined by the direction of the rapid movement with regard to the patient's right or left side. In other words, horizontal nystagmus to the left is one in which the rapid movement is directed horizontally to the patient's left side, is accentuated by turning the eyes to the left and is lessened or suppressed when gazing to the right. Rotary nystagmus is designated according to the direction of the upper end of the vertical iris meridian. It, too, is increased by voluntary movement of the eyes in the direction of rapid motion and attenuated by looking in the opposite direction.

The following signs will serve for the ready indication of the various forms of nystagmus:

- L. → Horizontal nystagmus to the left, increased on looking to the left.
- R. ← Horizontal nystagmus to the right, increased on looking to the right.
- L. ↶ Rotary nystagmus to the left, increased on looking to the left.
- R. ↷ Rotary nystagmus to the right, increased on looking to the right.
- U. ↑ Vertical nystagmus upward, increased on looking up.
- D. ↓ Vertical nystagmus downward, increased on looking down.
- D. R. ↙ Diagonal nystagmus to the right downward, increased by looking to the right downward.
- U. R. ↖ Diagonal nystagmus to the right upward, increased by looking to the right upward, etc.

TURNING NYSTAGMUS.

When the head is turned on a vertical axis to the right the endolymph in the right horizontal canal, *at the beginning of the rotation,* is displaced *toward the ampulla.* If we were to stand in a tram wagon and the same be suddenly set in

---

*The use of the terms right and left in designating direction of nystagmus always refers to the patient's right or left and never to that of the examiner.

motion we would fall backwards as a result of our own inertia; in like manner the endolymph remains stationary for a moment at the beginning of rotation. The movement of the endolymph must, of course, be microscopic in view of the diminutive size of the canal and the relatively great friction. *Should the rotation continue even a few seconds, the endolymph will come to a standstill in the tube and participate in the motion of the canal itself. But upon cessation of the turning movement the endolymph must cantinue a moment in the original direction as a result of its momentum, or, in other words, in this case in the direction *from the ampulla to the smooth end.*

---

*That the movement of the endolymph is only microscopic was proved by Neumann, who observed a case in which the posterior half of the horizontal canal had been accidentally chiseled away during the course of an operation. The patient was totally deaf immediately after the operation, but later gained a hearing power of whispered speech at nine meters. After the lapse of several weeks when revolved in the turning chair he developed a typical, though subnormal, horizontal nystagmus. This phenomenon, as well as the improved hearing, was due to the fact that the ampulla with its hair cells was intact, had become closed in the course of healing and again performed its functions but slightly hampered by the loss of the canal.

THE PHYSIOLOGY OF TURNING NYSTAGMUS.

By a nystagmus to the right is meant a slow movement of both eyes to the left and a *rapid return movement to the right—a nystagmus being designated according to the direction of the rapid movement.* What is the significance then of these two movements? One of these movements, let it be understood, is the direct result of some vestibular disturbance, the other is the effort of the individual to restore normal macular fixation. *The slow movement is the vestibular reflex, while the rapid movement is the voluntary movement back to the normal position.* The question at once arises as to what determines the direction of the nystagmic movement of the eyes, or, in other words, why a movement of the endolymph in the right horizontal canal from the smooth end toward the ampulla should result in a nystagmus to the right. An answer to this question constitutes the key to the whole physiology of the semicircular canals.

The ocular musculature is constantly in a condition of balanced tonus. Any disturbing influence emanating from either labyrinth will serve to upset this balance, resulting in ocular movement in one direction or another. Therefore either increased or diminished stimulation from either side will serve to disturb the tonic balance. Each labyrinth is, therefore, capable of producing a nystagmus in either direction.

When the head is turned to the right both horizontal canals are affected at the same time, and the endolymph is moved to the same degree. It would be reasonable to expect that the resulting stimulation would therefore be the same in each, and, if so, the ocular balance would not be disturbed and hence no nystagmus result. The fact is, however, that the stimulus produced is *not* the same. The efficiency of the stimulus depends upon the position or direction of the ampullary hairs. Ewald proved that:

1. *The ampullary hairs in the horizontal canals exercise the maximum stimulation when they are directed from the smooth end toward the ampulla and vice versa.* Fig. VI., A and B.

2. *The ampullary hairs in the vertical canals exercise the maximum stimulation when they are*

directed from the ampulla toward the smooth end and vice versa. Fig. VI., C and D.

The hair cells of the ampullæ are swayed like miniature seaweed by the endolymph current.

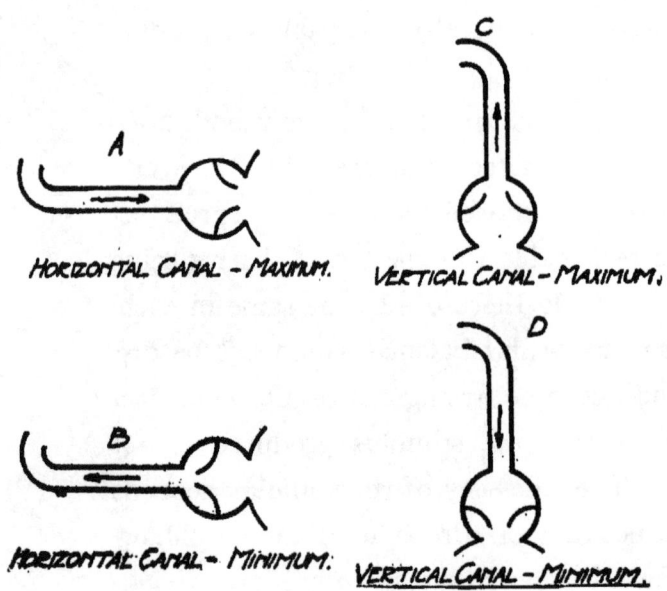

Figure VI. Schematic representation of horizontal and vertical canals showing position of ampullary hairs for maximum and minimum stimulation.

While the head is turning to the right, as we have seen, the endolymph in the right horizontal canal is displaced *from the smooth end toward the ampulla,* while the endolymph in the left horizontal canal is displaced *from the ampulla toward the smooth end*. The ampullary hairs are, therefore, in a position of maximum stimulation in the right canal and minimum stimulation in the left canal. Either of these two factors would suffice to upset the ocular equilibrium.

¶Finally, *each labyrinth stands in relationship to the adductor muscles of the same side and the abductor muscles of the opposite side.*

•Increased stimulation from the right side results in a contraction of the right abductors and left abductors which, with diminished stimulation to their opponents coming from the left labyrinth, results in a slow movement of the eyes to the left. This is followed by a rapid voluntary return to the normal position and we have a *horizontal nystagmus to the right*. Fig. VII.

¶This is the phenomenon observed *during* the turning process. If, however, after prolonged turning, the head be brought to a sudden standstill the endolymph current in each horizontal canal is reversed. As a result the ampullary hairs are placed in a position opposite to the one described. Increased stimulation now comes from the left labyrinth and diminished stimulation from the right. The left adductors and right abductors contract, the eyes move slowly to the

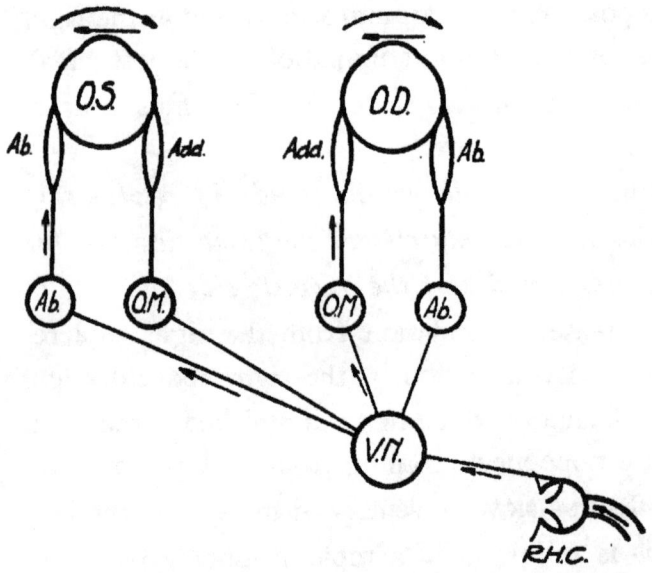

Figure VII. Schematic representation of the labyrinth and ocular muscles.
R. H. C—Right horizontal canal. V. N.—Vestibular nucleus. O. M.—Oculomotor center. Ab—Abducens center. Straight arrow indicates slow movement, curved arrow the rapid or voluntary nystagmic movement.

right with a rapid return to the left and we have a *horizontal after-nystagmus to the left.*

By means of rotation we are able to produce a nystagmus in any desired direction. The nystagmus during rotation as well as the after-nystagmus depends merely upon the *position of the head* during the turning.

If we consider the rotation of the head in the upright position we perceive that the endolymph in the horizontal canals is more especially affected. The degree to which the endolymph in any given canal is moved depends upon the relative angle of this canal to the horizontal plane (assuming always that the rotation be on a vertical axis). Should such a canal lie entirely in the horizontal plane the motion of the contained endolymph would reach its maximum. On the other hand, if the canal lies vertical to the horizontal plane, *i. e.*, in the axis of rotation, the motion of its endolymph will be nil.

The following law discovered by Flourens will serve to determine the direction of ocular excursions resulting from lymph movements: *Each semicircular canal evokes ocular movements in its respective plane. When several canals functionate simultaneously the resulting ocular excursions will be modified in accordance with the determining impulses.*

The law which determines the kind and direction of a nystagmus produced by turning on a vertical axis is as follows: *The line of intersection of a horizontal plane with the cornea will determine the kind of nystagmus, while the direction of rotation specifies the direction of the nystagmus during the act of rotation*, e. g., turning to the right with the head erect will produce a *horizontal* nystagmus to the right during the turning process. Inclining the head to the right shoulder at an angle of 90 degrees and turning to the right will result in a *vertical* nystagmus upward, *i. e.,* toward the patient's vertex. Bending the head forward at an angle of 90 degrees the horizontal plane will touch the cornea at a point, therefore, producing upon rotation to the right a *rotary* nystagmus to the right. Bending the head backwards at an angle of 90 degrees there results in like manner upon rotation to the right a *rotary* nystagmus in the same direction. (This is, however, in relation to the patient a rotary nystagmus to the left owing to the backward position of the head.)

In the positions of the head mesial to those

mentioned we obtain combination forms of nystagmus, *e. g.,* inclining the head forward at an angle of 45 degrees, there results a combination of horizontal and rotary nystagmus to the right; inclining the head backwards 45 degrees produces a combination of horizontal nystagmus to the right and rotary nystagmus to the left. Here we see the remarkable instance of nystagmus in opposite directions produced by turning, the horizontal nystagmus being increased by looking to the right, the rotary nystagmus by looking to the left.

CONCOMITANTS OF NYSTAGMUS—VERTIGO OF ROTATION.

The concomitants of nystagmus are partly subjective and partly objective in nature. Among the former are:

1st. An apparent movement of external objects depending upon the creation of optical impressions during the nystagmic excursions of the eyes. In view of the fact that a nystagmus is accentuated by vision in the direction of its rapid motion and lessened or suppressed by gazing in the direction of its slow motion, the apparent movement of external objects is increased or suspended in a like manner.

2d. The sensation of falling is frequently experienced with the eyes open and is the rule with the eyes closed. When the eyes are closed a look in the direction of the rapid excursion accentuates this sensation of falling, while looking in the opposite direction reduces or suspends it. (Barany.)

3d. Reactionary movements of the body: If during a rotary nystagmus to the right the individual stand in the position for the Romberg test with eyes closed and heels together, he will fall to the left. If the head be turned 90 degrees to the right he will fall forward, and if the head be turned 90 degrees to the left he will fall backward.

The law governing reactionary movements is as follows: *The movements of a body take place in the same plane with the nystagmus and in the direction opposite to the rapid nystagmic movement.*

Rotary nystagmus to the right is a nystagmus

in the *frontal* plane to the right, the head being in the upright position; the direction of reactionary movement in the frontal plane must, therefore, be to the left. Turning the upright head 90 degrees to the right the nystagmus will be in the sagittal plane and directed backward and the reactionary movement of the body in that plane forward. Inclining the head 90 degrees forward the nystagmus will be in the horizontal plane and the reactionary movement upon revolution to the left will produce no falling. In general *the reactionary movement produces a disturbance of equilibrium only when it does not take place in the horizontal plane according to the law above cited.*

4th. Not infrequently the individual experiences at the time of his nystagmus a darkening of the visual field, chromatopsia and scotoma scintillans.

5th. Horizontal nystagmus is seldom accompanied by nausea or vomiting except in cases of neurasthenia. Rotary and vertical nystagmus not infrequently induce nausea even in those of sound nerves, but especially is this true of neurasthenics.

6th. Pallor or blushing, sweat, palpitation or

slowing of the pulse, tremor, rapid and deep breathing are concomitants of rotary and vertical nystagmus, especially in nervous individuals.

7th. Some individuals retain consciousness during nystagmus, while in others there is a slight loss of consciousness, which, in rare cases, may even become complete; the latter again applies to neurasthenics.

All of the phenomena mentioned under these seven heads constitute our conception of the vertigo of rotation. A loss of orientation appears to be combined with vertigo only in cases exhibiting a partial loss of consciousness.

METHOD OF CONDUCTING THE TURNING TEST.

In testing for turning nystagmus the patient is seated in a revolving chair similar to a desk chair turning on a swivel. A pair of spectacles fitted with opaque lenses is next fitted in position before the eyes for the purpose of eliminating the physiological optical nystagmus (already described) resulting from the altering visual fixation during the revolving process. He is then rotated ten times at a uniform speed.

In this manner Barany examined approximately two hundred individuals and arrived at the following conclusions:

1. That there exists a very considerable variation in the duration of the after-nystagmus under physiological conditions.

2. That there apparently exists no constant relationship between the nystagmus and the rapidity with which the patient was revolved in the chair.

3. That variations in age exhibited no difference as to the average duration of horizontal nystagmus.

4. That ten revolutions produced on an average the most pronounced nystagmus.

5. That neurasthenia apparently prolonged the duration of horizontal nystagmus.

6. That in the case of dancers, who, while dancing, habitually turn to the right there is an appreciable decrease in the duration of horizontal nystagmus to the left, while the rotary nystagmus showed no variation from the normal.

Because of the lack of a suitable turn-table for the examination of individuals *during* the process of turning, a number of such investigations were conducted on a carousal, and showed that the simultaneous nystagmus varies in duration quite as much as does the after-nystagmus.

The cessation of nystagmus during prolonged revolution and the phenomenon of after-nystagmus has been varyingly explained. The following seems reasonable. The primary movement of the endolymph and the consequent irritation of the hair cells when the revolution is begun results in the discharge of latent nerve impulses from Deiter's area. This discharge may be sudden or gradual, according to conditions, resulting in either a rapid and radical or a slower and lesser nystagmus. When the stored impulses have become exhausted the eyes will remain quiescent during continued revolution. At the moment of cessation the other center which effects a nystagmus in the opposite direction discharges its impulses, bringing about an opposite after-nystagmus of a different duration.

The acceptance of two vestibular centers (*e. g.*, in Deiter's area), which serve to maintain a constant vestibular tonus of the ocular muscles and a normal equilibrium while at rest, cannot be denied. The after-nystagmus and its greater rapidity and intensity following prolonged rotation, as well as the greater duration of the horizontal as compared to vertical nystagmus, may all be plausibly explained as being of central origin.

CALORIC NYSTAGMUS.

In the year 1868 Schmiedekam and Hensen discovered that the introduction of cold water into the external auditory canal resulted in vertigo, nausea and vomiting, while water at body temperature produced none of these effects. Many aurists had also noticed that irrigating with too hot or too cold water produced vertigo and nystagmus. About three years ago Barany, Ruttin and Neumann, began investigations regarding caloric nystagmus, and arrived at the following conclusions: If water at a temperature lower than that of the body be injected into the right ear of an individual whose vestibular apparatus is intact, there results a horizontal and rotary nystagmus to the left. If the injected water be of a temperature higher than that of the body, there results a rotary nystagmus to the right. If cold water be injected into the right ear and the head be inverted there again results a rotary nystagmus to the right. Therefore, the effect of hot water injected into the ear with the head in the upright position is the same as that of cold water with the head inverted.

This phenomenon may be explained on a basis of physical laws, as follows: Consider the labyrinth as a vessel filled with liquid at a temperature of 37 degrees C. If a stream of cold water be directed against the outer wall of such a vessel, the contained fluid lying in contact with the wall becomes cold and sinks to the lowest level of the vessel. In this way there results a circulation in the vessel which in the case of the labyrinth would, however, be almost microscopic. Obviously, if a stream of hot water be employed the resulting currents will be in the opposite direction.

The only question which now remains to be answered is why irrigation of the right ear with cold water should result in a rotary nystagmus to the left, the head being in the upright position. When the head is erect the arch of the anterior vertical canal constitutes the highest point of the labyrinth, while the ampulla of the same canal lies in apposition with the outer wall of the internal ear. If a stream of cold water be directed against the outer wall of the right labyrinth, the endolymph will move from the arch of the canal downward toward the ampulla. This places the ampullary hairs in a position of least effective stimulation; the normal complement from the left labyrinth overbalances this, resulting in a *rotary nystagmus to the left.*

Of importance also is the observation of the nystagmus when inclining the head to the right or left shoulder. Irrigating the right ear with cold water and inclining the head to the left shoulder results in a *horizontal* nystagmus to the right; if the head be inclined to the right shoulder there follows a horizontal nystagmus to the left. This may be explained as follows: When the head is inclined to the left shoulder, the horizontal semi-circular canal lies in the vertical position. Its arch constitutes the highest point of the vestibule, and the ampulla lies in contact with the anterior wall. If cold water be injected against this wall the endolymph current set up in the horizontal canal is directed from the arch toward the ampulla. This is the same current set up by turning the upright head to the right resulting in a horizontal nystagmus to the right during the turning process.

CALORIC REACTION IN DIAGNOSIS.

The caloric reactions above described are found in every case in which the vestibular apparatus is intact, irrespective of the presence or absence of the tympanic membrane. If the labyrinthine temperature is above normal, these reactions can be demonstrated only by the use of water of still lower temperature. If the vestibular apparatus be destroyed or the vestibular nerve paralyzed, no nystagmus can be produced on the affected side by the use of either cold or hot water. We are, therefore, enabled to diagnose unilateral destruction of the vestibular apparatus providing the vestibular nerve is intact. There are exceptional cases in which this method fails, *e. g.,* cases of pronounced atresia of the external canal or those in which a collection of cholesteatomatous masses interfere with the injection of water. Furthermore, cases of severe inflammation of the middle ear, on account of the increased bodily heat, respond only to the prolonged injection of very cold water. The method may be employed with impunity in all cases excepting those of traumatic rupture or dry perforation of the tympanic membrane, and in such cases a current of cold air may be substituted.

Before conducting the test the patient should be examined for the presence of spontaneous nystagmus. This having been excluded water of a temperature of 30 degrees C. is injected into the ear by means of an ordinary fountain syringe equipped with a small tube or catheter, the patient being seated on a chair or in a semi-upright position in bed.* The ordinary ear syringe is not adapted to this purpose owing to its limited capacity. If no nystagmus is established the temperature of the water may be reduced to 20 degrees C., or even lower. Should the patient exhibit a spontaneous nystagmus he must be instructed to fix his

---

*The specially constructed irrigator devised by Ruttin offers distinct advantages for this test.

gaze in such a direction that the nystagmus disappears, or will at least be minimal; the test then proceeds, the injected water being below 20 degrees C. It is in just such cases affected with a spontaneous nystagmus that the test must be conducted with the greatest precision, for the life of the patient not infrequently depends upon the correct examination of the caloric nystagmus.

NYSTAGMUS RESULTING FROM COMPRESSION AND RAREFACTION OF THE AIR IN THE EXTERNAL AUDITORY CANAL—FISTULA TEST.

This form of nystagmus is found in cases affected with a fistula in the lateral labyrinthine wall. As a result of the compression and rarefaction of the air the endolymph is put in motion, thereby producing a nystagmus. If the vestibular apparatus shows a normal irritability, gradual excursions of the eyes will be produced and a rapid nystagmus of several seconds duration. Even if the vestibular apparatus shows little or no irritability for cold water slight motions may be induced by this method because of the greater stimulation.

It is true that very slight ocular movements have been observed as a result of compression and rarefaction in the absence of a labyrinthine fistula. But in these cases the eye movements resulting from the caloric test are very slight, and it is just this absence of pronounced difference between the caloric reaction and that of compression which precludes the presence of a fistula. The ocular movements resulting from compression and rarefaction vary in their direction in different cases, although that following compression is always opposite to that resulting from rarefaction.

This test may be carried out by means of a Politzer bag equipped with an olive tip fitting air tight into the canal. The examiner must stand close to the patient in order to observe the slight ocular excursions, the patient fixing his gaze directly forward.

GALVANIC NYSTAGMUS.

Volta was the first to observe the fact that a lateral galvanism of the head resulted in vertigo and disturbed equilibrium, but it remained for

Hitzig, in the year 1870, to discover galvanic nystagmus. Since that time a large number of investigations have confirmed and amplified his work.

If the cathode be applied to the right ear there results a rotary nystagmus to the right, while the anode applied to the same ear produces a rotary nystagmus to the left. Galvanic nystagmus can be seen most readily when the eyes occupy the extreme position in the direction of the rapid movement. This form of rotary nystagmus like every other is accompanied by vertigo and disturbed equilibrium.

To explain galvanic nystagmus we must recall the fact that the cathode induces a catelectrotonus in the affected nerve. This serves not only as an irritant but enhances the conductivity of the nerve so that peripheral impulses become more effective. Breuer assumed a gradual continual flow of endolymph in both labyrinths resulting in constant stimuli to the centers. This flow of the endolymph being uniform on both sides in the state of rest, the resulting auto-stimulation maintains a state of equilibrium. Even though we might not subscribe to this hypothesis we cannot deny the assumption of continued and symmetrical stimuli. We may consider the vestibular

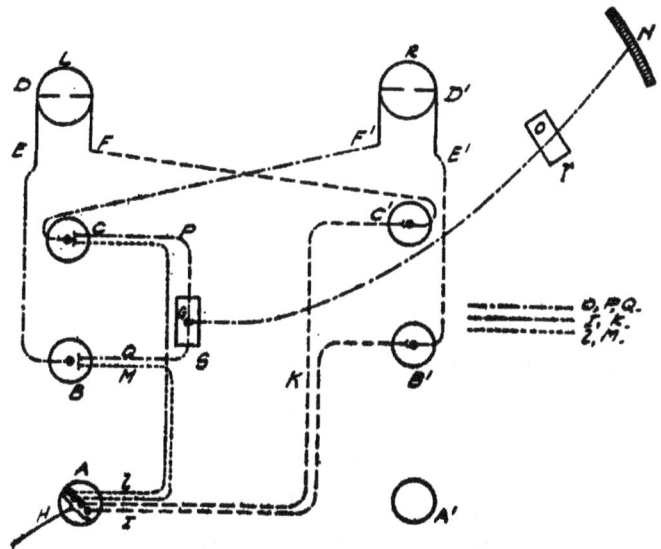

Figure VIII. Schematic representation of left horizontal nystagmus originating in the left labyrinth. (After Barany).
A, A'—Deiter's nuclei. B, B'—Nuclei of abducens. C, C'—Nuclei of motor oculi. D, D'—Left and right eye. E, E'—External recti muscles. F, F'—Internal recti muscles. H—Vestibular nerve. I—Route of impulses to contralateral abducens nucleus. K—Route of impulses to contralateral motor oculi nucleus. L and M—Route of inhibitory impulses to nuclei of abducens and motor oculi of the same side. N—Right cortical center for voluntary ocular movement to the left. P—Supranuclear tract from left visual center to oculomotor area of the same side. Q—Supranuclear tract from left visual center to abducens area of the same side.

ganglion as the source of these stimuli, and assume that the impulses coming from the right labyrinth induce the slow movement of a nystagmus to the right, while the left labyrinth effects a slow movement of a nystagmus to the left. Fig. VIII. In consequence of the symmetrical stimulation both eyes remain at rest, their muscles being in a state of vestibular tonus. Only on this basis can the effect of the anode be explained. Anelectrotonus reduces the conductivity of a nerve with the result that peripheral stimuli are inhibited, the impulses of the opposite side predominating and producing the opposite form of nystagmus.

No great practical importance as yet attaches to galvanic nystagmus for the following reasons: In cases which fail to respond to the caloric or compression tests a galvanic reaction could be established which could scarcely be differentiated from that of the normal side; furthermore, it has been possible to produce a typical nystagmus by introducing an electrode into the cavity of an extirpated labyrinth. It must be assumed in these cases that the nystagmus originated either in the nerve itself or else in Deiter's area.

ACUTE DESTRUCTION OF THE LABYRINTH.

We find acute destruction of the labyrinth in acute purulent labyrinthitis, in labyrinthine hæmorrhages as a result of arteriosclerosis, in leukemia, syphilis and fractures at the base of the skull. The symptoms are in all cases the same. Immediately following the injury there results in both eyes a violent rotary and horizontal nystagmus toward the unaffected side accompanied by severe vertigo, apparent movement of external objects as well as of the body, nausea and vomiting, great disturbances of equilibrium and inability to walk. The patients are compelled to lie down and always assume a typical position, namely, upon the sound side. This is explained by the fact that the patient can view his surroundings only by directing his eyes toward the affected side in which position the nystagmus as well as the subjective concomitants are minimal. Nothing will induce such a patient to look toward the unaffected side whereby his nystagmus would become most violent. If such a patient be examined for the caloric and compression reaction the spontaneous nystagmus will be found to be unaffected by these tests, thus establishing the diagnosis of labyrinth destruction.

The violent phenomena above described usually continue for two or three days after which the nystagmus gradually decreases. In individuals with sound nervous systems the subjective symptoms disappear before the nystagmus. Even on the third day following the destructive process vertigo is no longer experienced in the resting position while the nystagmus continues to a considerable degree. Only when the head is suddenly turned and the nystagmus increased is the vertigo re-established.

It is remarkable to note that the nystagmus disappears much more rapidly after extirpation of the labyrinth than when the diseased organ is left untouched. This may be due to the fact that although the end organ no longer responds to caloric and mechanical stimulation, pathological irritation is carried to the nerve center, which is less capable of adapting itself to the altered condition than when these pathological stimuli cease as a result of operation. Not infrequently following the cessation of nystagmus to the sound side a supervening horizontal nystagmus to the affected side may be noted. This phenomenon has not yet been explained.

In elucidating the manifestations following acute destruction of the labyrinth we must refer to the explanation of galvanic nystagmus. We may compare the destruction of the labyrinth to the action of the anode. If the right labyrinth be suddenly removed the impulses coming from the left labyrinth predominate and there results a nystagmus to the sound side induced principally by the unaffected labyrinth.

After the lapse of two or three weeks following the destructive process all of the symptoms resulting therefrom will have disappeared with the exception of a faint nystagmus in either direction, and we now have the picture of latent labyrinthine destruction. In these cases the diagnosis can be made only by means of the caloric reaction or eventually by the turning test.

In the majority of cases the caloric test will suffice, no variation being noted in the spontaneous nystagmus as a result of the test. Cases in which cholesteatomatous masses or severe acute inflammatory processes render the caloric reaction doubtful must then be subjected to the rotation test.

VERTIGO.

Circumscribed affections of the vestibular apparatus are characterized by normal reaction to the caloric and rotary tests and by spontaneous attacks of vertigo. The latter are of two kinds:

(1) Those which appear without any external cause while walking, eating, writing or even during sleep. These spontaneous attacks are, as a rule, severe and long lasting, are usually attended by nystagmus to the affected side and occasionally even to the sound side. Such attacks may last from one-half hour to several hours, the patient during the intervening periods being apparently well and showing no signs of nystagmus or disturbed equilibration.

(2) The second form of vertigo depends on external causes, such as rapid movement of the head, stooping and sudden assumption of the erect position, bending the head backwards especially towards the affected side, passing from a

cold to a warm room or vice versa; and, as a result of alcohol, nicotine or intestinal intoxication. These attacks are likewise accompanied by nystagmus but seldom by nausea. The vertigo is not severe and lasts from a few seconds to several minutes. Cochlear symptoms may be found accompanying both forms of vertigo.

Both forms of vertigo are found in cases of labyrinthine fistula resulting from acute and chronic middle ear suppurations. In such cases we may find pronounced deafness or tinnitus or both. If the seat of the disease process producing the vertigo lies in the course of the vestibular nerve between its peripheral ending and its entrance to the medulla oblongata we may expect to find also disturbances of the cochlea. But if the lesion lies within the medulla oblongata and in the region of the posterior longitudinal bundle as far as the oculo-motor centers, acoustic disturbances will be wanting.

Slight attacks of vertigo of the second type may also be caused by circulatory disturbances, and are seldom accompanied by either tinnitus or deafness. The vertigo found in arterio-sclerosis of the small cerebral vessels and in connection with the menopause is chiefly of circulatory origin.

Of toxic origin is the vertigo of smokers and those afflicted with gastro-intestinal diseases. Furthermore, we find attacks of dizziness in normal individuals, *e. g.,* when suddenly rising from a recumbent position or rapidly stooping forward. Neurasthenics very frequently complain of vertigo. They are unable to fix their gaze upon a given point for any length of time, an attempt to do so resulting in dizziness and a tendency to fall. The effort at fixed vision is accompanied by a constant unrest of the eyes resulting in an apparent movement of external objects.

The attacks of vertigo found in accident cases are of special practical importance. Nearly every patient suffering from an injury to the skull complains of vertigo. If we take a careful history of these cases we will be able to divide them into two groups. One of these will be composed of those cases in whom the loss of consciousness was followed by vertigo which lasted several days and was increased by every motion of the head. Such a history is characteristic of destruction of the labyrinth, and an examination will establish an existing deafness and a lack of irritability of the vestibular apparatus.

The patients in the second group complain of no vertigo so long as they remain in bed; their vertigo begins when they leave the bed, reoccuring during any rapid movement, on suddenly arising, stooping or even spontaneously without any external cause. These cases show a normal response to the caloric and rotation tests. Tinnitus and bilateral deafness are frequently observed, although there are cases of vertigo without attending cochlear disturbances.

Patients of the second class are frequently afflicted with nausea and vomiting. They become very anxious and excited, pale or flushed and exhibit at such times profuse perspiration, palpitation, violent headaches, general tremors, partial loss of consciousness and syncope. Having received this history of a case we proceed with the rotation test for horizontal nystagmus. This is usually negative. We then test for rotary nystagmus, and, as a rule, obtain a reaction of such distinctness that there remains no doubt as to the diagnosis.

It will be readily understood how the sudden and unlooked for attacks while at work or on the street serve to render the patient fearful and to bring about a lack of confidence. Such patients are easily excited and exhibit even between attacks an uncertain and rolling gait, together with typical neurasthenic symptoms.

INDICATIONS FOR LABYRINTHINE OPERATION IN ACUTE DIFFUSE, LATENT DIFFUSE AND CIRCUMSCRIBED LABYRINTHINE SUPPURATIONS.

However small the amount of pus contained in a purulent labyrinth, it none the less endangers the cranial contents. It is quite analogous in its significance to appendicitis with regard to the abdomen. Left to itself a purulent labyrinthitis may in time heal spontaneously, the pus becoming sequestered, the contained micro-organisms losing their virulence, and the exudate becoming organized, fibrous or calcareous. In a large percentage of cases, however, purulent affections of the labyrinth result in grave intra-cranial complications, cerebral abscess and meningitis.

In view of the large mortality among cases of purulent labyrinthine disease we are in duty bound to resort to operative procedures in every instance except those in which the general condition of the patient precludes all interference. This is especially true when we consider that labyrinthine operations are not particularly severe or dangerous (Politzer). It remains for us to consider the indications which determine the time and manner of operative interference.

ACUTE DIFFUSE LABYRINTH SUPPURATION.

Given a patient exhibiting the symptoms of acute purulent labyrinthine disease, we proceed as follows: (1) If the patient exhibits such symptoms as fever, headache, foul discharge, pain in region of the mastoid, or periosteal abscess we must operate at once. (2) If the patient exhibit no symptoms necessitating immediate intervention we may treat the case on the expectant plan in the hope that the pus may become walled off from the cranial contents and then combine the mastoid operation with extirpation of the labyrinth at the end of eight or ten days.

LATENT DIFFUSE LABYRINTH SUPPURATION.

Given a patient in whom an examination establishes a latent form of purulent labyrinthitis the mastoid operation must, in every case, be extended to include the labyrinth, for failure to do so very frequently results in post-operative meningitis.

CIRCUMSCRIBED LABYRINTH SUPPURATION.

The indications in cases of circumscribed purulent disease of the labyrinth are more involved. To understand these more fully we must first consider the possible courses of this condition. In the first place the radical mastoid operation must be performed in all such cases. As sequelæ we may have: (1) Gradual resolution of the purulent process without further interference, the labyrinthine fistula becoming closed by granulation tissue which may become fibrous or even osseous. Such cases may even be relieved of their vertigo, although frequent attacks of vertigo, more or less severe, will supervene after the lapse of years. (2) An extention of the circumscribed condition resulting in a *diffuse* form of purulent labyrinthitis with all its attendant dangers.

Operative interference is, therefore, to be considered in circumscribed purulent labyrinthitis as well, inasmuch as the choice may lie between the danger of the diffuse form on one hand and spontaneous healing with protracted invalidism on the other. Our decision will depend on the state of the patient's hearing. If the unaffected ear be normal and the diseased ear quite deaf we are justified in advising the operation. Should the affected ear still retain good hearing and the other ear be quite deaf, we are not justified in undertaking the operation, and in opening the mastoid must take special precaution to guard against interference with the existing fistula.

The operation on the labyrinth includes the total extirpation of the semicircular canals and the free opening of the vestibule and cochlea. Failure to open the vestibule and cochlea is quite as dangerous as the omission of the operation itself. In performing this operation apply the chisel vertically to the rear half of the horizontal canal and then remove everything which lies posterior to this line. It is often necessary to open the sinus, the posterior and frequently, also, the middle cerebral fossa in order to gain sufficient room and permit inspection and drainage. Whenever possible after opening the vestibule the lateral wall of the inner ear is also removed. This done the cochlea is opened at the promontory. When this operation has been completed a probe directed backward from the oval window must appear in the vestibule.

NYSTAGMUS OF INTRA-CRANIAL ORIGIN.

We have noted above that vertigo and nystagmus may originate not only in the peripheral end organ of the vestibular nerve but also in its intra-cranial course. The differential diagnosis depends largely upon the presence or absence of accompanying cochlear symptoms, and in case of the normal irritability of the vestibular apparatus, on the participation of the other cerebral nerves. In those cases in which the vestibular apparatus has lost its irritability, a positive diagnosis may be made based on the kind of spontaneus nystagmus existing. If the right vestibular apparatus is not responsive and there is observed a strong rotary nystagmus to the right, such a nystagmus is due to intra-cranial disease.

This may be explained as follows: Each labyrinth when irritated produces a nystagmus toward the same side. When a labyrinth is paralyzed it is no longer capable of producing a nystagmus toward the affected side. When such a nystagmus exists, it must, therefore, be due to intra-cranial irritation of either the vestibular nerve or of Deiter's area.

If the right vestibular apparatus is destroyed and there exists a rotary nystagmus to the left, we should immediately look for its origin in the left labyrinth, but as we have learned, such a nystagmus must show a continual decline from the first moment of observation. If this is not the case and the nystagmus shows an increasing intensity it is of intra-cranial origin. Such a diagnosis is made more easily when, in cases of chronic purulent disease with loss of labyrinthine irritability, we have previously performed a radical operation and extirpated the labyrinth. In such cases the labyrinthine nystagmus toward the sound side will disappear almost completely in from three to four days. If, on the other hand, the nystagmus continues or increases, we may with certainty regard it as of intra-cranial origin.

Meningitis of the posterior cerebral fossa and cerebellar abscess are the principal intra-cranial causes of nystagmus observed in cases of chronic middle ear disease. In the event of a chronic purulent condition in which the tympanic membrane is normal but with nystagmus of the described type and a lack of vestibular irritability, a diagnosis of tumor in the region of the acoustic nerve is most probable. Such a symptom complex, accompanied as it usually is by deafness, constitutes a valuable indication for the early diagnosis of such tumors.

The following tables condensed from Mackenzie will serve as a ready guide in differential diagnosis:

TABLE I.

LABYRINTH SUPPURATION.	PERILABYRINTHITIS.
1.—More often secondary to chronic middle ear suppuration.	1.—More often secondary to acute middle ear suppuration.
2.—The process begins suddenly.	2.—The process is more gradual.
3.—May be associated with mastoiditis.	3.—Always associated with mastoiditis.
4.—Otoscopic findings not characteristic.	4.—Otoscopic findings in advanced cases always show necrotic bone.
5.—Associate facial palsy the exception.	5.—Facial palsy the rule.
6.—As a rule, associated meningeal irritation, meningitis or other intra-cranial complicatons.	6.—Intracranial complications the exceptions.
7.—No direct relationship to systemic or constitutional diseases.	7.—Frequent association of systemic or constitutional diseases.
8.—The Weber test shows lateralization to the well ear.	8.—Weber lateralized to the diseased ear. (Neumann.)

TABLE II.

LABYRINTH SUPPURATION.	NEURITIS OF EIGHTH NERVE.
1.—Positive history of middle ear suppuration, together with the history of previous attacks of vertigo.	1.—Negative history of middle ear suppuration; but on the contrary history of infectious disease, or some toxic poisoning (quinine, salicyates, alcohol, tobacco, etc.), or exposure to cold and moisture.

2.—Otoscopic findings characteristic for middle ear suppuration (secretion, perforation, polyps, cholesteatoma, etc.).	2.—Otoscopic findings negative in cases of herpes zoster involving the membrana tympani.
3.—Tinnitus and subjective noises negative.	3.—Tinnitus and subjective noises usually positive.
4.—Deafness is absolute.	4.—Deafness may be absolute or partial.
5.—Intense vertigo lasting from three to five days.	5.—Intense vertigo lasting, as a rule, longer than in the case of labyrinth suppuration.
6.—Spontaneous rotary nystagmus to the sound side.	6.—Same as in labyrinth suppuration.
7.—Negative caloric irritability.	7.—Same as in labyrnth suppuration.
8.—Paresis of other cranial nerves rarely.	8.—Paresis of other cranial nerves.
9.—Unilateral involvement.	9.—Frequently bilateral.
10.—Permanent loss of both acoustic and static functions.	10.—Recovery of both acoustic and static functions.

TABLE III.

LABYRINTH SUPPURATION.	CEREBELLAR ABSCESS.
1.—Absolute deafness of sudden onset.	1.—Positive hearing.
2.—Vertigo intense at first but constantly diminishing.	2.—Vertigo less intense, but increasing.
3.—Pronounced spontaneous rotary nystagmus to the well side in the early stages, but profuse in intensity.	3.—Sponetaneous horizontal nystagmus to the diseased side or rotary to either, but more often to the diseased side, increasing in intensity.

4.—Equilibrium disturbances and tendency to fall to the diseased side, less intense but increasing.	4.—Equilibrium disturbances with tendency to fall to the diseased side, marked at first but diminishing.
5.—Reaction of the static labyrinth positive.	5.—Reaction of the static labyrinth negative.
6.—Positive symptoms of cerebellar abscess; localized, occipital tenderness, rigidity of the neck, homolateral hemi-paresis and hemianæsthesia, cerebellar ataxia, optic neuritis or choked disc, impairment of intellect (slow cerebration), great loss of body weight, bradycardia.	6.—No symptoms of cerebellar abscess.
7.—Removal of the labyrinth not indicated.	7.—Removal oi the labyrinth is followed by improvement.